# JALISCO & SANTA

BY KAYDEN PHOENIX

Andrews McMeel Publishing
a division of Andrews McMeel Universal
1130 Walnut Street, Kansas City, Missouri 64106
www.andrewsmcmeel.com

25 26 27 28 29 SDB 10 9 8 7 6 5 4 3 2 1

Paperback ISBN: 978-1-5248-9258-6
Hardcover ISBN: 978-1-5248-9259-3
Library of Congress Control Number: 2024948420

## Jalisco

Written by **KAYDEN PHOENIX**
Art by **AMANDA JULINA GONZALEZ**
Inking by **HANNAH DIAZ**
Coloring by **MIRELLE ORTEGA, ADDY RIVERA SONDA, GLORIA FELIX**
Lettering by **SANDRA ROMERO**

## Santa

Written by **KAYDEN PHOENIX**
Art by **EVA CABRERA**
Color by **GLORIA FELIX**
Lettering and design by **SANDRA ROMERO**

Editor: Hannah Kimber
Art Director: Jessica Rodriguez
Production Editor: Elizabeth A. Garcia
Production Manager: Jeff Preuss

Made by:
RR Donnelley (Guangdong) Printing Solutions Company Ltd.
Address and location of manufacturer:
No. 2, Minzhu Road, Daning, Humen Town,
Dongguan City, Guangdong Province, China 523930
1st Printing – 2/10/25

# JALISCO

CHAPTER 1 .......... 3
CHAPTER 2 .......... 13
CHAPTER 3 .......... 23
CHAPTER 4 .......... 29
CHAPTER 5 .......... 35
CHAPTER 6 .......... 43

# SANTA

CHAPTER 1 .......... 63
CHAPTER 2 .......... 73
CHAPTER 3 .......... 81
CHAPTER 4 .......... 91
CHAPTER 5 .......... 101
CHAPTER 6 .......... 111

JALISCO

Chapter 1

GUADALAJARA

LOVELY AFTERNOON, SEÑORA ALVAREZ.

CARNICERÍA
"PORKY"
UMMM, HELLO?!

EXCUSE ME, SEÑOR ANTONIO.

CHOP

GET OUT !!!
THIS SHOP IS FOR PAYING CUSTOMERS.

PLEASE, TOÑO. WE NEED FOOD, AND ORITO ISN'T HAVING THE BEST SEASON...
...BUT THEY'RE REALLY GOOD.

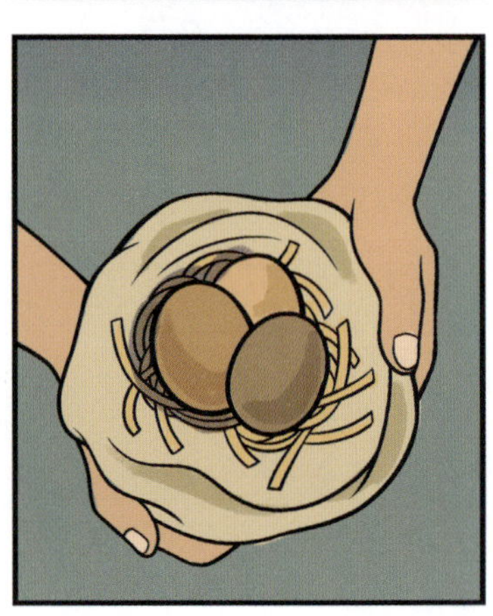

EGGS DON'T PAY THE BILLS. NOW SHOO!!

YO, TOÑO! FREEZER AIN'T WORKING BACK HERE!

WHAT?!?

I DUNNO, I KICKED IT AND–

YOU KICKED THE FREEZER?!?

YEAH, TO MAKE IT WORK.
AYE, OK, WATCH THE STORE.

IMMA LEAVE THIS RIGHT HERE ON THE COUNTER. IF IT DISAPPEARS, I KNOW NOTHING.
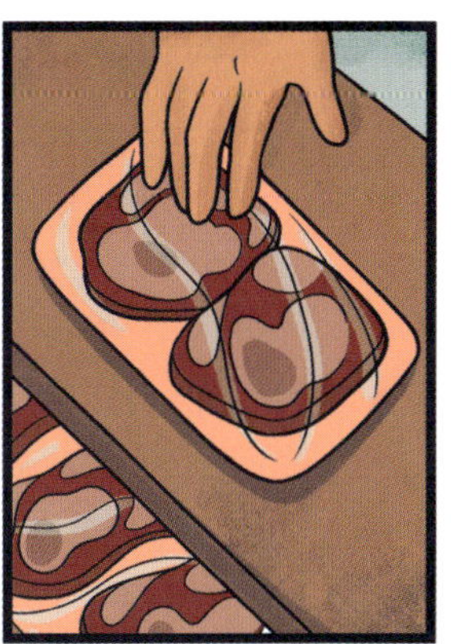
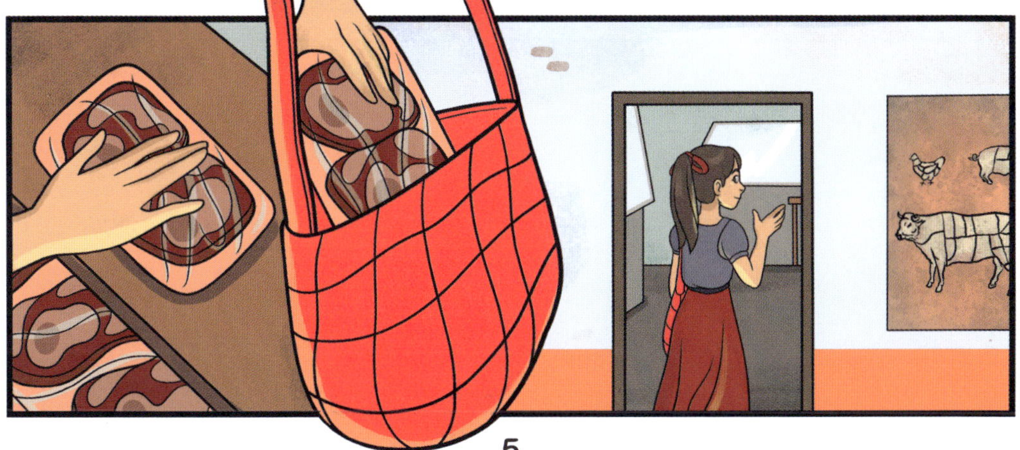

HEY, ORITO.
I BROUGHT YOU SOMETHING.

AND THIS IS FOR MA.

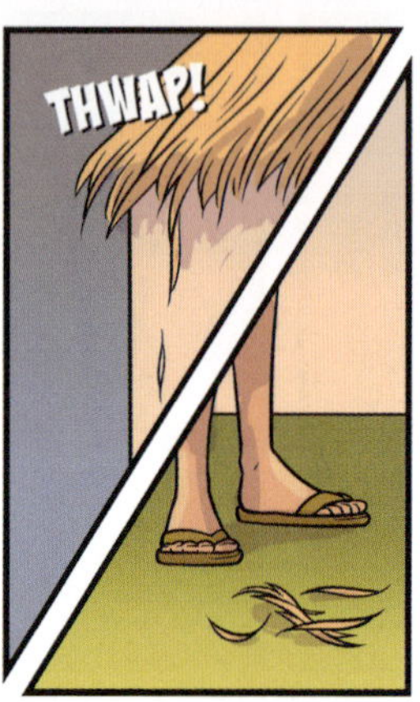
THWAP!

I GOTTA FIX THAT.

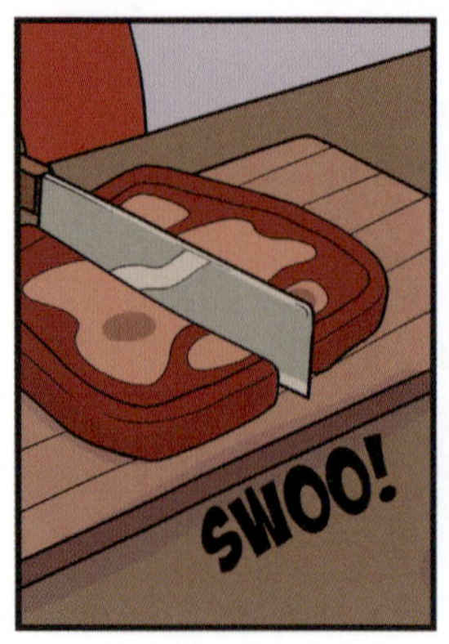
SWOO!

SWOO!

CLICK!

HI, MOM,
I GOT YOU
SOMETHING!

ALICIA, DUMPSTER
DIVING IS NOT SAFE!
NO, MA, I GOT
THIS AT THE
CARNECERÍA.

THEY GAVE
IT TO ME
FOR FREE!

UH HUH...
...AND THOSE?

THOSE ARE FROM THE DUMPSTER.
THE FOOD'S ALMOST READY.
YOU SHOULD GO RELAX.
HOW WAS WORK?
ANYTHING GOOD?
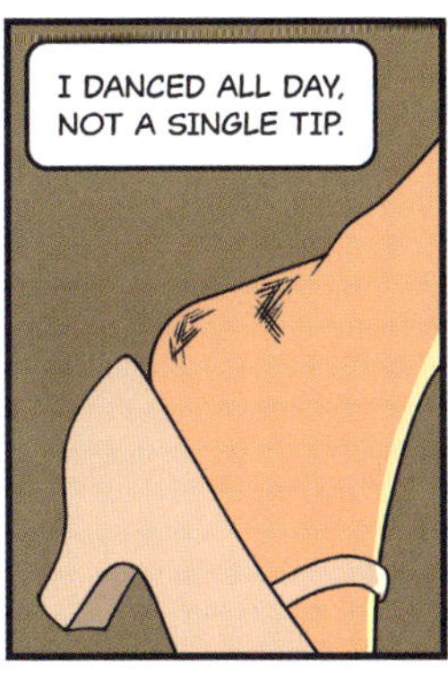
I DANCED ALL DAY,
NOT A SINGLE TIP.

YOU SHOULD
STOP.
MY FEET HURT...
BUT I HAVE TO
KEEP DANCING.

HEY, DON'T BE SO GLUM.
WE GOT MEAT BECAUSE
OF YOU. AND YOU GOT
ME FLOWERS...

...KINDA...
YEAH.

YOU WANT TO GO TO THE
PARK LIKE WE USED TO? I
WANT TO SEE YOU DANCE.
YOU STILL REMEMBER?
OF COURSE I DO!
YOU TAUGHT ME.
UH HUH.
GO PUT
ON MY
SHOES.

DON'T LET ANYONE EVER TELL YOU THAT YOU CAN'T BARTER WITH EGGS.

OK, MA.

YOU READY TO DANCE, ALICIA?

YEAH.

WHICH DANCE?
DANCE JARABE. MY FAVORITE.
MA, I KNOW. BUT WHICH SONG?

ANY. JUST DANCE JALISCO.

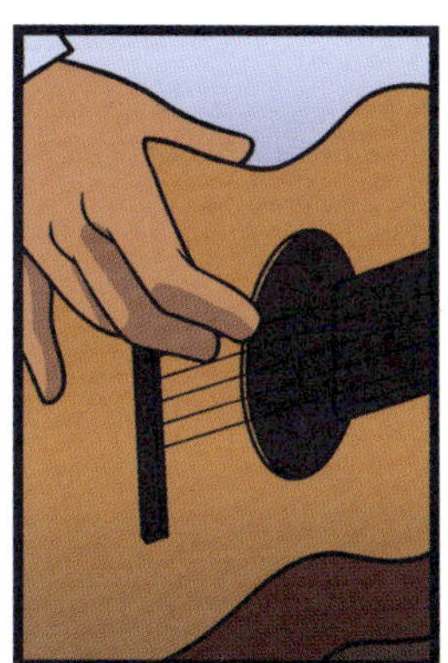

EXCUSE ME, SEÑORITA?

ONLY FOR THE MOST BEAUTIFUL GIRLS IN TOWN.

AND ONE FOR MY...

MA? MA!

WHERE IS SHE?
WHO, SEÑORITA?
MY MOM. *SHE WAS HERE!*
LO SIENTO, SEÑORITA, I SAW NO ONE.
SHE WAS RIGHT HERE!

*MA!*

SIR, PLEASE, YOU HAVE TO HELP ME!
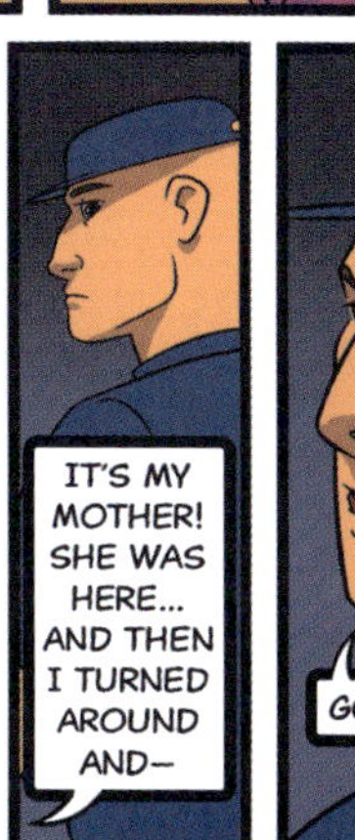
IT'S MY MOTHER! SHE WAS HERE... AND THEN I TURNED AROUND AND—

GO HOME.

YOU'RE LUCKY THEY DIDN'T TAKE YOU TOO.

TAKE?
WHO?

MA, ARE YOU HERE?

SQUAWK

THIS ISN'T FOR YOU, ORITO!
I'M NOT SURE WHO THIS IS FOR.

OTRA VEZ, MIJITA!
OK, MA!

BRAVO!

PAPA! YOU'RE HOME!

THWAP!

GOTTA FIX THAT WHILE THERE'S STILL LIGHT...

...AND A ROOF.
WANT TO HELP ME FIX THE ROOF?
YEAH!

GO GET MY KNIFE!

OK!

SHE'S A BABY. WHAT IF SHE FALLS?
WE ALL HAVE TO LEARN THINGS THE HARD WAY SOMETIMES.
HERE YOU GO, PAPA!

WE GOTTA PROTECT OUR HOME AT ALL TIMES. RIGHT, MIJA?

YOU GOTTA BUY A DRINK TO BE IN HERE.

UHH, JUST A COKE, PLEASE.

EVERYONE!
CAN I GET YOUR ATTENTION, PLEASE?
MY NAME IS ALICIA CUEVAS. I LIVE RIGHT OUTSIDE GUADALAJARA WITH MY MOM. TONIGHT, SHE WAS TAKEN. PLEASE, CAN SOMEONE HELP ME FIND HER?

ZZZZ

PTOOEY!

I JUST WANT TO FIND HER.

OH! *WAIT!*

*WHAT THE HELL?!* THIS *ISN'T* PAYMENT!

PHREEEEET!

POW!

Chapter 2

HAPPY BIRTHDAY, BABY. IT'S TIME TO WAKE UP.

JUST A LITTLE LONGER?

HAPPY BIRTHDAY!
PAPA!
COUGH! COUGH!

I NEED TO FIND MY MA!

HE WANTS TO SPEAK TO YOU, BABY.

DON'T GO, PAPA.
I'M JUST SLEEPING FOR A WHILE, MIJA. WHEN I WAKE UP AGAIN, WE'LL WALK THE STREETS AND SAY HI TO EVERYONE TOGETHER.
HOLD MY HAND, MIJA.
WHO ARE YOU?
WHERE AM I? WHY DID YOU—
YOU WERE OUT FOR A WHILE THERE.
I SAVED YOU. YOU'RE WELCOME.
WHERE ARE YOU GOING? YOU DIDN'T TELL ME WHY I'M HERE! PLEASE, LET ME GO!

CREAK!

OH, YOU CAME–

I'M RAQUEL, BUT EVERYONE CALLS ME ROCKY.

SORRY FOR ALL THE MYSTERY.

THAT'S DELLA FOR YOU.
SHE TAKES HER JOB TOO SERIOUSLY SOMETIMES.

I DON'T KNOW WHERE I AM. I'M FROM TALA.

HMM... NOT FAMILIAR WITH IT.
WHAT STATE ARE YOU FROM?

JALISCO.

I DON'T KNOW WHERE THAT IS, BUT YOU'LL BE *JALISCO* SO I DON'T FORGET IT. COME ON!

WAIT! WHY AM I HERE?
HEY, RELAX, JALISCO. IT'S COOL. YOU'RE SAFE HERE.
*WHERE?!* WHERE AM I?
YOU'RE IN CHIHUAHUA NOW.

WANT A DRINK? FOOD? WE HAVE POZOLE FROM LAST NIGHT.
JUST WATER, PLEASE. MY HEAD STILL HURTS.

THERE'S A BUMP.
GUESS I GOT HIT HARDER THAN I THOUGHT.

THAT'S JUST LIKE HER. KNOW WHY THAT IS?
BECAUSE SHE CAN GET AWAY WITH IT, THAT'S WHY.

SHE'S THE DAUGHTER OF THE ELDEST, ADELLA. YOU'LL MEET HER SOON.

*WHAT?!*
WHO?
WHY?

ADELLA.
SHE'S DELLA'S MOM... AND THE BOSS.

YOU'LL LOVE HER.

SHE'S THE LAST LIVING ADELITA: REVOLUTIONARIES IN THE MEXICAN—
I KNOW WHO THEY ARE.

THERE'S A LOT GOING ON OUT THERE. *SHE* IS GETTING STRONGER. AND I GUESS IT HAS SPREAD TO JALISCO NOW, TOO, WHERE DELLA FOUND YOU.
AND YOU? WHAT DO YOU DO?
SAME AS YOU, I GUESS. I WAS AN ORPHAN. ADELLA WAS IN MONTERREY, MY HOMETOWN. SHE RAISED ME LIKE ONE OF HER OWN. BUT SHE HASN'T PUT ME IN THE FIELD YET.
I HAVE TO PROVE MYSELF, YOU KNOW?
NO.
I DON'T UNDERSTAND.
CLICK!
CLACK!
SHE'S COMING.
DELLA!
ADELLA?
ADELITA!
I'M SO CONFUSED.
I'M ADELLA SANTOS DE LAS ADELITAS.
NICE TO MEET YOU.
WELCOME HOME, SEÑORITA.

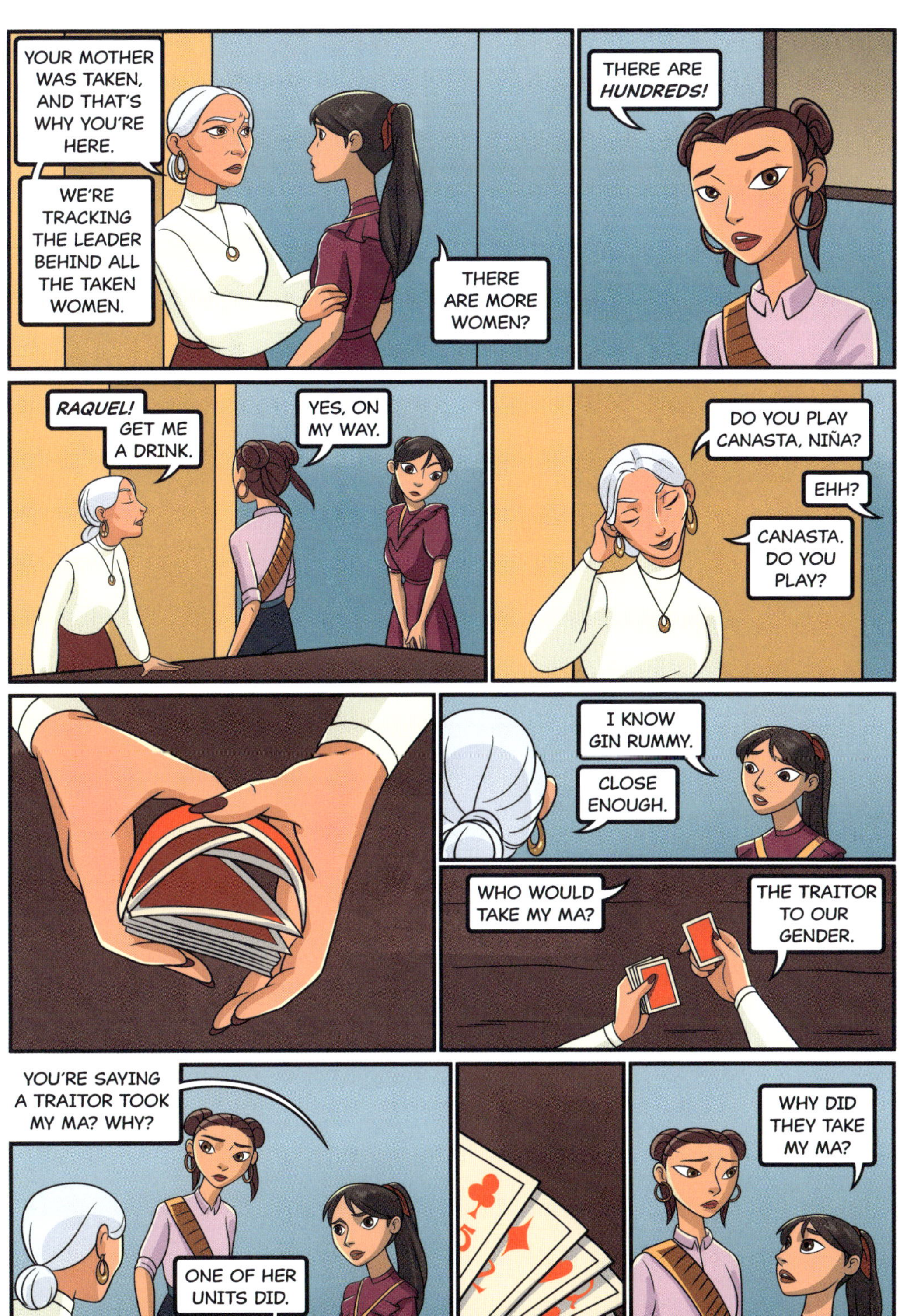
YOUR MOTHER WAS TAKEN, AND THAT'S WHY YOU'RE HERE.
WE'RE TRACKING THE LEADER BEHIND ALL THE TAKEN WOMEN.
THERE ARE MORE WOMEN?
THERE ARE *HUNDREDS!*
*RAQUEL!* GET ME A DRINK.
YES, ON MY WAY.
DO YOU PLAY CANASTA, NIÑA?
EHH?
CANASTA. DO YOU PLAY?
I KNOW GIN RUMMY.
CLOSE ENOUGH.
WHO WOULD TAKE MY MA?
THE TRAITOR TO OUR GENDER.
YOU'RE SAYING A TRAITOR TOOK MY MA? WHY?
ONE OF HER UNITS DID.
THANKS, RAQUEL.
WHY DID THEY TAKE MY MA?

THEY CHOOSE RANDOM WOMEN THROUGHOUT CHIHUAHUA. TO GET INITIATED, THE LOYALISTS HAVE TO BRING SOMEONE TO THE TRAITOR FROM OUTSIDE OF—

YA, RAQUEL!

WAIT, WHAT? TELL ME WHAT THEY HAVE TO DO!
IT'S YOUR TURN. PLAY!

DELLA BROUGHT YOU HERE FOR YOUR PROTECTION.

IF YOU CHOOSE, YOU CAN HELP BRING THE TRAITOR DOWN.
WHO?

MALINCHE.

LATER THAT DAY...
YOU'LL NEED TRAINING.
WHAT KIND?
DID YOU GO TO SCHOOL?
A LITTLE.
DO YOU HAVE ANY SKILLS?
LIKE?
WHAT DID YOU DO BACK HOME?
UMM... I DANCED.

SEE THAT?

WHO IS THAT?
THEY TEND NOT TO IDENTIFY THEM.

I WANT TO FIND MY MOM, NOT SEE DEAD GIRLS...

NO ONE WANTS TO SEE DEAD GIRLS, MIJA.

HOW'D YOU KNOW THAT GIRL WAS HERE?

THEY DUMP THEM HERE SOMETIMES.
WHAT'S THAT LADY'S PROBLEM?
CÁLMATE. THEY CAN HEAR YOU.

COME ON.

I HAVE TO RUN AN ERRAND. WE'RE GOING TO THE TAILOR SHOP.

*NIÑA!*

YES?
LEAVE HER ALONE.
WHO?

YOU WILL UNDERSTAND WHEN YOU ARE READY.
VÁMONOS. WE'RE GOING TO START YOUR TRAINING.

DAY 1 OF TRAINING
WHOAH.

GET IN THE RING. IT'S TIME YOU LEARNED TO TAKE A PUNCH.

I DON'T THINK THIS IS GOING TO BE A FAIR FIGHT.

YOU THINK ANY FIGHT IS?
BLOCK.
DON'T HELP HER!

BAM
FINISH THE FIGHT!
WHAT KIND OF TRAINING IS THIS?

SORRY.

WHAM

ARE YOU DEAD?
...I'M STILL HERE.

Chapter 3

GOOD. THEN GET BACK UP!

BAM

DAY 2 OF TRAINING
HMM, MAYBE YOU'RE BETTER WITH WEAPONS.

BREAK IT AND EVERYTHING INSIDE IS YOURS.

BAM
BAM
BAM

POOF!

I DIDN'T KNOW I COULD DO THAT!

DAY 3 OF TRAINING
DEFEND YOURSELF.

CLINK!
CLINK!
WHOOSH!

INTERESTING.
STRIKE HER!

NO!
CLINK!
CLINK!
CLANG
WHAT TYPE OF DANCING DID YOU SAY?
FOLKLÓRICO.
WHICH SCHOOL?
I DIDN'T GO TO SCHOOL.
WHERE DID YOU LEARN?
MY MOM.
I'M SURE SHE TAUGHT YOU WELL.
I WANT YOU TO SHOW ME.
HOLD IT LIKE THIS.
YOUR FEET... IT'S LIKE TAP DANCING.
WHAT DO YOU DO WITH YOUR ARMS?
AND IF YOU TURN SLOWY...
CHOP
WHY ARE WE CUTTING ALL THESE POTATOES?
ADELLA'S BIRTHDAY IS TONIGHT. EVERYONE'S COMING OVER.
WHO'S EVERYONE?

I'M DELIGHTED YOU'RE ALL HERE.

WE WERE WAITING FOR YOU.
I'M SORRY. I WASN'T SURE WHAT TO WEAR.

WE DIDN'T GIVE YOU TIME TO PACK.
I NEED YOU TO TAKE A NOTE TO PASQUELITA'S. REMEMBER THE TAILOR SHOP?

NO ONE HAS COME BACK.
WHAT?
YOU'LL BE AN ORPHAN, LIKE RAQUEL.

NO!
MY MOM'S ALIVE!
AND I'M GONNA FIND HER!

THERE ONCE WAS A LITTLE NIÑA.

SHE LOVED TO PLAY IN THE SUN. ONE DAY, SHE FELL ASLEEP OUTSIDE AND GOT BURNED. THE KIDS MADE FUN OF HER.

HER MOM SAID IT WAS KISSES FROM GOD, BUT IT WAS TOO LATE. THE NIÑA TURNED DARK INSIDE, DEEP WITHIN HER SOUL. HER JEALOUSY OVERTOOK HER, AND NOW SHE TAKES THE LIGHT FROM EVERY NIÑA SHE FINDS.

THAT'S A HORRIBLE STORY.
THAT'S MALINCHE'S STORY.

I'M SORRY I RUINED YOUR PARTY.

IT'S NOT A PARTY UNLESS ALL MY GIRLS ARE THERE.
COME ON, DO YOU KNOW HOW TO LIGHT FIREWORKS?

NO.
YOU'LL PICK IT UP.

Chapter 4
NI UNA MÁS

Pasquelita's
CLOSED
HMM.
ita's

NO! LEAVE ME ALONE!!
MALINCHE!

STOP!

BAM!

LET GO OF HER!

LET–GO–OF–HER!

ÁNDALE, PUES.
¡LÁRGATE!

RUN!

YOU LOOK DIFFERENT FROM THE OTHERS.
WHERE ARE YOU FROM?

JALISCO.
WHERE'S MY MOM?

AY, NIÑA.

PLEASE. SHE'S THE ONLY FAMILY I HAVE.
I WON'T TELL ADELLA.

EEK!

ADELLA CAN'T HELP YOU.

HE- H- HELP!
PATHETIC LITTLE GIRL. YOU CAN'T EVEN FIGHT.

ENOUGH!

SCREEEECH

THUMP

PUNCH ME!
ADELLA ISN'T HERE...
JUST DO IT!
FINE. BUT I'M NOT APOLOGIZING THIS TIME.

POW!!

OW, THAT HURT.

WERE YOU EXPECTING SOMETHING DIFFERENT? HERE.

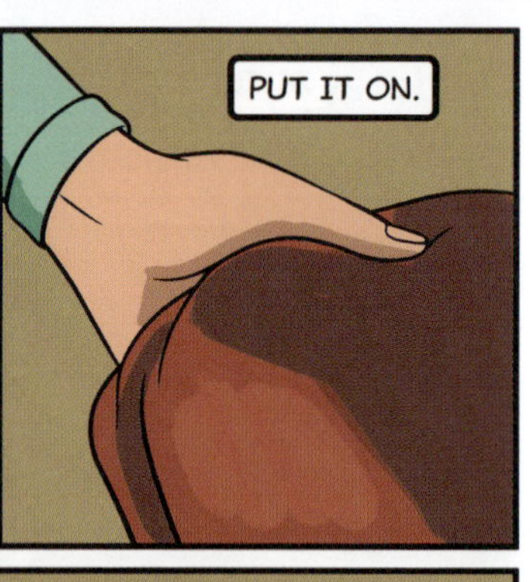
PUT IT ON.

NOW WHAT?
NOW, YOU FIGHT.
I CAN'T MOVE IN THIS.

HOLD IT HOW YOU DO WHEN YOU DANCE.

THE FABRIC, IT'S REALLY THIC-

PUNCH HER!

*WHAT?*
*NO!*

THUMP!

¿VISTE? AGAIN!

USE THE SARAPE.
THAT'S IT?

DON'T GET HIT, OR YOU'LL DIE.
WAIT, WHY DO I HAVE THESE?
DEFENSE.

RUN.
AHHHHH!

CRACK!

OK, THINK.
DEFENSE.
THE SARAPE.

AH!

DEFEND YOURSELF!
THAT'S THE POINT OF THIS EXERCISE!
HOW?

WE'RE SUPPOSED TO STAY STILL!
SHH...

MA, YOU CHEATED!
NO BABY, I WAS JUST USING WHAT I HAVE. USE EVERYTHING TO YOUR ADVANTAGE.

TINK!

RUN!

TINK!

TINK!

TINK!
H-HAA!

Chapter 5

MA, IT'S BEEN A COUPLE OF MONTHS.
I'M GONNA FIND YOU, I PROMISE.

I'M JUST A GIRL, WITHOUT YOU, MA.

I'M JUST *NIÑA*. NOBODY KNOWS MY NAME. I'M JUST *JALISCO* TO THEM.

YOU'RE HERE FOR ME?

I HAVEN'T CHANGED. I'M STILL ME.
YES, I'M ME. I'M ALICIA.
I'M NOT A DIFFERENT PERSON.

DANCE JARABE, ALICIA.
MA, I KNOW. BUT WHICH SONG?

ANY. JUST DANCE JALISCO.

JALISCO.

SIGH.
WHEN WILL THIS END?

WHAT ARE WE GOING TO DO?

WHAT DO YOU SUGGEST?

HEY!
CAN I WALK YOU HOME?

WILL YOU TEACH ME THAT DANCE?
THIS IS AIKIDO. IT IS A FLOW, NIÑA. TRY TO PUNCH ME.
I WON'T PUNCH YOU.
I KNOW, JUST TRY.

WHOOSH!
SLAM!

I WASN'T EXPECTING THIS.
PRECISELY. NOW YOU TRY.

YOU *NEVER* TAUGHT ME THIS! *I* SHOULD KNOW THIS, AS YOUR DAUGHTER. NOT THIS... THIS...

¡CÁLMATE!
NIÑA, WILL YOU LEAVE US FOR A MOMENT?
SURE.

WOULD YOU SAVE YOUR SISTER IF GIVEN THE CHANCE?
I DON'T HAVE A SISTER.

SAY YOU DID, AND YOUR MOM TREATED HER DIFFERENTLY BECAUSE OF HER SKIN TONE. WOULD YOU DEFEND HER?
UM, YEAH, I GUESS.

AGAINST YOUR OWN MOTHER?
AGAINST ANYONE.
WHY?
BECAUSE... SHE'S MY SISTER, A HUMAN BEING. AND HER SKIN COLOR DOESN'T MATTER.

ALWAYS HELP THOSE WHO NEED DEFENDING, ESPECIALLY LITTLE SISTERS.
WHO IS YOUR SISTER, MOM?

I HAD A SISTER WHO USED TO PLAY IN THE SUN. SHE HAD...
...THE PRETTIEST HAIR. IT GLISTENED...

THEY'VE BEEN QUITE STUBBORN ABOUT WALKING THEM HOME AFTER WORK.

WHAT DO YOU PROPOSE?
WE TAKE THEM FROM THEIR HOMES.
THE CHIQUILLAS ARE TOO EASY.
THEN WHAT?

IT'S TIME WE MAKE HEADLINES.

NIÑAS?
YOU'RE EARLY.

WELL WELL, IF IT AIN'T THE ANCIENT ADELITA.

IF YOU LET ME KNOW WHY YOU ARE HERE, I WILL HELP YOU GET ON YOUR WAY.
OOH, SHE'S GOT MANNERS.
BUT DOES SHE HAVE ALL HER TEETH?

LET'S SEE. SMILE FOR THE CAMERA!

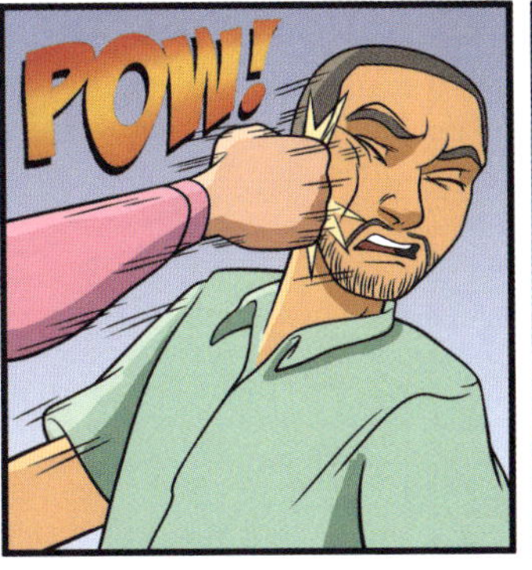
POW!

AY, PAYASO.
YOU KNOW, MALINCHE WARNED US ABOUT YOU. YOU'RE A FIGHTER.
AT LEAST SOMEONE'S SMART.

RIGHT, AND THAT'S WHY THERE ARE MORE OF US.

FLICK!
CRRR!
BAM
POW

ARRRG!
SENIOR CITIZEN!
WHOOSH!
JUST ADMIT DEFEAT.
YOU LOST.

I'M NOT DEAD YET.

¿YA TE VAS?
NOT YET.

THERE ARE MORE OF US.

IMAGINE A MILLION OF US! WE COULD SAVE SO MANY!
WAIT...

FIRE!

WHY WOULD THEY DO THIS?

BAGAAAW!

NO.

NO!
NO, *PLEASE!*

MA? NO!

I'M SO SORRY, MA.

Chapter 6

THM!
THM!

THM!
THM!

GOD, OUR FATHER, WE ENTRUST ADELLA SANTOS, LAST LIVING ADELITA OF THE MEXICAN REVOLUTION, INTO YOUR HANDS. SHE WAS A NOBLE SPIRIT, A PROTECTOR. WE HUMBLY ASK THAT YOU TAKE HER INTO YOUR KINGDOM.

I DON'T KNOW HOW TO SEND YOU OFF, MA.
I GOT YOU A FLOWER, SO WHEN YOU'RE SLEEPING, YOU'LL THINK OF ME.

JALISCO, WAKE UP.

HERE.

I'M SORRY I DIDN'T COME TO ADELLA'S FUNERAL.
IT'S OK, I GET IT.

MY MOM WAS A FIGHTER...

...LIKE YOURS.

SHE WAS HAVING THIS MADE FOR YOU.

JALISCO

never
waste
your
pain

AY!

HMMM.

ADELLA!

I'M GONNA MAKE THINGS RIGHT.

I PROMISE.

HEY, WAIT UP! I HAVE AN IDEA...

SOOO...
YOU WANT ME TO GO WITH YOU TWO...

A GIRL WHO JUST LEARNED TO FIGHT.

AND YOU, A TRAINER WHO HAS NEVER BEEN OUT IN THE FIELD.

TO KILL MALINCHE.
YES.
ARE YOU IN?

EXCUSE ME!
IF I CAN HAVE THE FLOOR, PLEASE.

EVERYONE, LISTEN UP!

I'M JALISCO. I WAS FORTUNATE TO KNOW ADELLA. SHE HELPED TRANSFORM ME INTO A BETTER PERSON. A FIGHTER. AN ADELITA.

AS ADELITAS, WE DON'T STAND FOR INJUSTICES. WE ARE WARRIORS. WE FIGHT FOR WOMEN.

I HAVE A PLAN TO TAKE DOWN MALINCHE.

WHAT ARE YOU GOING TO DO, WALK IN AND KILL HER?

RIGHT THROUGH THE MISSION'S FRONT DOORS?

THAT IS EXACTLY WHAT I PLAN TO DO.

WE'RE GOING TO INFILTRATE THE MISSION. ANY HELP IS WELCOME.
WE LEAVE TONIGHT.

ANY IDEA HOW WE'RE GONNA GET IN?
THE FRONT DOORS.

GOOD ONE.
OKAY, I HAVE AN IDEA THAT MIGHT WORK. SEE THAT BELL TOWER? IF WE GO AROUND AND UP...

OYE!

SHE WAS SERIOUS.
LET'S RECALCULATE.

FIRE AT WILL.

HEY, ROCKY,
WANT TO ALERT THE OTHERS INSTEAD? IF WE'RE NOT A TEAM, WE'RE NOTHING, RIGHT?
TWEET
PERFECT.
CLICK
PEW!
PEW!
PEW!
DING!
DING!
DING!
TWEET
TWEET

BAM!

PEW!
PEW!

PEW!
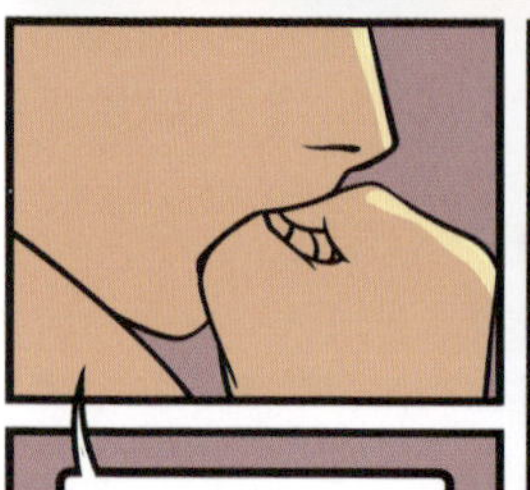

PSSST!

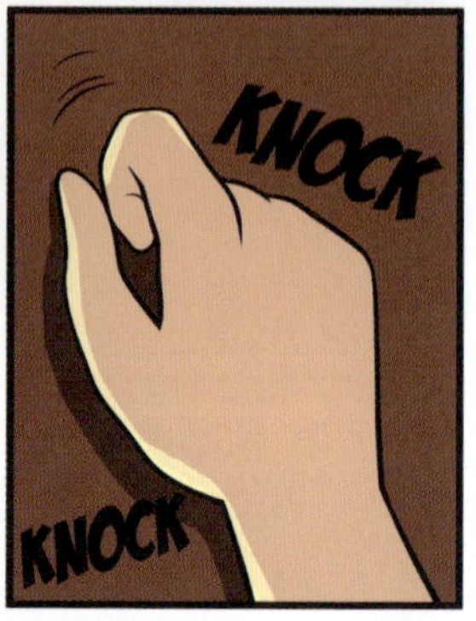
KNOCK
KNOCK

KEEP YOUR HANDS UP AND COME WITH ME!

SLAM!

NOW WHAT?
NOW, WE WAIT.

CREEEEEEK

WHY DID YOU COME HERE?

I'M HERE TO KILL YOU.
YEAH? YOU AND WHAT ARMY?
THEY'RE OUTSIDE WAITING.

WHY DO THEY WEAR MASKS?

BECAUSE THEY ARE IRRELEVANT. ANY MORE QUESTIONS, MOCOSA?

MAY I DANCE FOR YOU?

CLIP!
CLOP!
CLIP!
CLOP!

ATTACK!

CLICK!
WHOOSH!
POW!!
POW

BAM

NO! GUARDS!

ARRRG!

HELP THE OTHERS.

I GOT THIS.

MANO A MANO?

CLACK!
YOUR TURN, HERMANA.
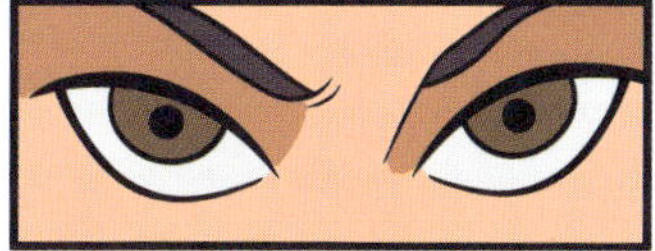

CLACK!

WHAT, NO WORDS OF CHIVALRY?
YOU WOULDN'T UNDERSTAND ANYWAY.
RIGHT.
DON'T WASTE YOUR BREATH.

BAM
POW

DID NO ONE SHOW YOU HOW TO DEFEND YOURSELF AGAINST THESE?

CHK-CHK

COME, ALICIA.
OK, MA!
LET ME SHOW YOU A NEW DANCE.

SOMETIMES WE DANCE OPPOSITE.
MEANING SOMETIMES YOU'RE A CHARRO, SOMETIMES YOU'RE AN ESCARAMUZA.

WE DANCE FOR EACH OTHER.
NEVER FORGET IT.
YOU LEARN THIS INSIDE AND OUT.

YES, MA!

TING!
TING!
PEW!
DANCE YOUR WAY OUT OF THIS.

BANG!
CLINK!

CLINK!
CLINK!

I'M SLIGHTLY IMPRESSED.
I'M HERE TO KILL YOU.

YOU'RE NOT A FIGHTER.
THAT'S WHY THEY GAVE YOU A FUNNY LITTLE DRESS.

SOMTHING NEW.
SOMETHING YOUR MOM COULD NEVER GIVE YOU.

CLASP!
SHWOOSH!

BAM
I MADE MY MEN LEAVE YOUR MOM WHERE I KNEW YOU'D FIND HER."

THUD!

WHOOSH!
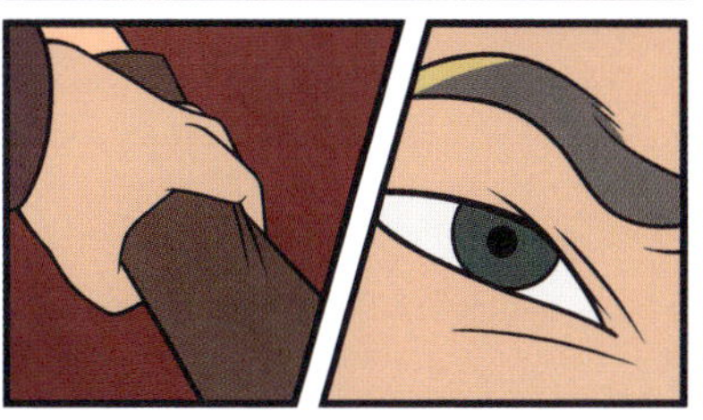

THUD!

LAST CALL FOR WORDS OF WISDOM.
CHK-CHK

NOOO!

POW

BAM!
BAM!
BAM!

ROCKY! YOU'RE OKAY... YOU HAVE TO BE OKAY...
I TRIED TO BE STRONG.

YOU ARE STRONG.
NO, ADELLA DIDN'T—
YOU WERE HER FAVORITE, YA KNOW?
THAT'S WHY SHE KEPT YOU BY HER SIDE.

I TRIED TO BE STRONG, LIKE YOU.
YOU'RE STRONG, ROCKY, YOU ARE! YOU ARE AN ADELITA!

CLANK!

SHWOOP!

STOP!

NO ONE CARES FOR YOU.
YOU'RE WEAK. A BRUISED LITTLE PEASANT GIRL THAT'S SAD ABOUT HER MOM'S MEANINGLESS DEATH.

AND THAT'S WHY I'M STRONGER THAN YOU.

DINK
DINK
KLGH!
KLGH!

CLANK!

IT'S DONE. MALINCHE IS DEAD.
WHERE'S ROCKY?

WE HAVE TO GET THE GIRLS OUT.

THREE DAYS LATER

# Santa

Chapter 1

OH NO!
GREAT!
HOW AM I SUPPOSED TO PAY FOR THIS?
HUH?!
CRAP!
AAAAAYY
HUH?!
WHAT ELSE CAN YOU THROW AT ME!
ARM WRESTLING TOURNAMENT
ARM WRESTLING TOURNAMENT
TO NIGHT
CHALLENGE ACCEPTED.

GO!
GO!
GO!
LUCHA
TOUGH CROWD, HUH?
TALKATIVE TYPE. OK... I'LL HAVE A WATER.
WE DON'T SERVE WATER HERE!
I JUST WANT TO DRINK SO I CAN GO ARM WRESTLE AND WIN SOME MONEY.
I'LL GET YOU SOMETHING TO DRINK, HONEY!
WHAT'S YOUR NAME?
NO THANKS.
BEAT IT! SHE'S *MINE!*
SAYS WHO?
SAYS ME?
LOS TÉCNICOS!
LOS ATÓMICOS!

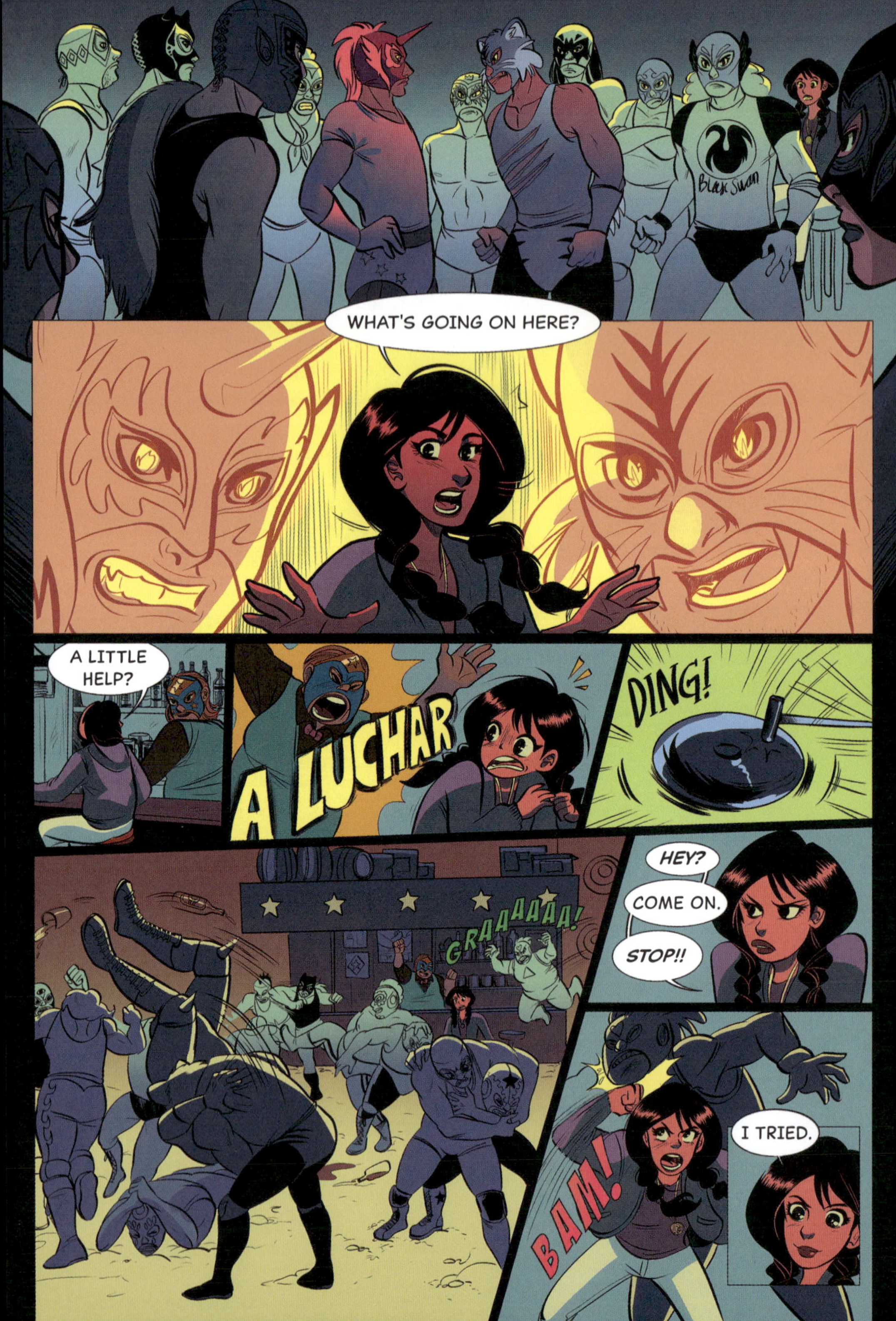
Black Swan
WHAT'S GOING ON HERE?
A LITTLE HELP?
A LUCHAR
DING!
GRAAAAAA!
HEY?
COME ON.
STOP!!
BAM!
I TRIED.

WHAM
CRACK
SLAM
WHERE WERE WE? OH YES, YOU ASKED MY NAME...
SANTA!
WHAT ARE YOU DOING WATCHING THAT?!
YOU SHOULD BE CLEANING! THE STORE IS A MESS!
THIS IS THE LAST STRAW. YOU'RE **FIRED**! GET UP AND GO HOME.
OH NO!
AGH! GREAT!!
HOW AM I SUPPOSED TO PAY FOR THIS?
HUH?!

AYY!
OH NO!
NO! NO! NO!
CRACK
CRAP!!
NOT AGAIN!
ARM WRESTLING TOURNAMENT
BUT I DON'T KNOW HOW TO FIGHT...
City of WEXO
You're Among Friends
WHRRRRRR
*COUGH*
*COUGH*
MIJA, QUE PASO?
I'M FINE, NANA, I JUST DON'T HAVE *IT*.
¿NO TIENES QUE?
IT'S LIKE THE WORLD'S AGAINST ME. NO PHONE, NO CAR, NO JOB.

THOSE ARE ALL REPLACEABLE. LOOK AT THE POSITIVE SIDE.
WHAT'S POSITIVE ABOUT ANY OF THAT?

NO ONE CAN KILL YOUR SPIRIT, SANTA.

YOU HUNGRY? GO CHANGE. LET'S GET SOME FOOD.
YES! I'LL BE RIGHT BACK.

OH...

DON'T FORGET THE KETCHUP, SANTITA!
OK!

GONZA BURGER

HEY!!

I'M SORRY. I'LL BUY YOU—OH... WAIT. I'M BROKE. I CAN'T... BUT I CAN OWE YOU—

DON'T WORRY ABOUT IT.
I SHOULD BE EATING HEALTHIER ANYWAY.

I'LL HAVE...

LINE'S BACK THERE.
OH! SORRY...

...AND YOU CAN WAIT IN LINE 'TIL WE'RE DONE, CHICA.

ALL GOOD HERE?
STAY OUT OF THIS. I GOT NO BEEF WITH YOU.
NEITHER DOES SHE. I'M SURE SHE DOESN'T MIND WAITING IN LINE.

IGNORE HER, RUCA.
COME ON. I'LL STAND WITH YOU. MY NAME IS COMADRE, BY THE WAY.
I'M SANTA.

WOW, WHERE'D YOU GET THAT PENDANT?
IT WAS MY MOM'S.

IT REMINDS ME OF MY PENDANT!
HEY, YOU SHOULD COME WORK IN THE CAMPAIGN OFFICE WITH ME.

THANKS, BUT I DON'T SPEAK POLITICS.
WE CAN TEACH YOU.

WE DON'T SERVE YOUR KIND HERE!
WHAT?!
LEAVE, BEFORE I CALL THE COPS.

I CAME TO GET MY GRANDMA HER FOOD!

IS EVERYTHING OK, MIJA?

GONZA BURGER
VÁMONOS, SANTITA.

SANTA?
WHAT HAPPENED AT SCHOOL, BABY?

YOU CAN TELL ME. I'LL BEAT ANYONE UP FOR YOU.
WELL?
THEY CALLED ME A WITCH, MOM.

OH YEAH?
YEAH

WELL, MAYBE YOU ARE A WITCH... LET ME SEE...
YES, IT SEEMS YOU ARE A WITCH!

SANTA, YOU CAN'T TELL ANYBODY. I THINK YOU GET IT FROM YOUR MOM.

I'M A WITCH?! I HAVE POWERS! RIGHT?
WE'LL PRACTICE YOUR POWERS WHEN I GET BACK.
YOU'RE LEAVING?
IT'S JUST FOR A LITTLE WHILE, BABY.

BUT WHAT IF THEY MAKE FUN OF ME AND I DON'T HAVE MY POWERS TO FIGHT THEM?

THIS IS YOUR AMULET, OK?
YOU HAVE YOUR WORDS AND THEY'RE STRONGER THAN ANYTHING. BUT, THIS WILL PROTECT YOU 'TIL I GET BACK.
WHY'D YOU HAVE TO GO?
YOUR MOM WAS A FIGHTER. IF SOMEONE NEEDED PROTECTING, SHE'D DO IT WITHOUT QUESTION.
THAT CASHIER AT GONZA'S DIDN'T LIKE US. WHAT KIND OF NATION IS THAT?
ONE THAT NEEDS FIXING.
BUT SHE DIED.
SANTITA, SOME THINGS ARE WORTH DYING FOR.
I GOTTA LEARN HOW TO FIGHT.
GATE G
CAMPAIGN OFFICE
DOÑA ACEVEDO

Chapter 2
VOTA
LA POLITICA
VOTE
LA POLITICA
VOTE
×
LA POLITICA
DONA ACEVEDO

LA POLITICA
DOMINOES
La Politica
DONA A
I'M GONNA DO JUST FINE HERE. YOU'LL SEE.
PULL
BAM!
YOU OK?
LA POLITICA
COMADRE INVITED ME.
WE SPEAK WEXAN HERE, NOT XICA.
STOP, AMBER.
SHE WAS KIDDING.
YOU MUST BE SANTA. ARE YOU A FIGHTER FOR THE PEOPLE?
UH, YEAH.
GREAT!
THAT'S THE PHONE BANK!
WE NEED TO REGISTER AND MOBILIZE VOTERS, PARTICULARLY NEW ONES.
VOTE DONA ACEVEDO FOR MAYOR
La Politica DONA ACEVEDO FOR MAYOR
VOTE x LA POLITICA
WE WANT THEM TO VOTE FOR ME.
FOR MAYOR
OTHERWISE KNOWN AS LA POLITICA.
YOU SEE THAT?
THE BILL OF RIGHTS.
Bill of Rights
PRIDE
AROUND THE WORLD
ALL POWER TO ALL THE PEOPLE
#MMIW
STOP KILLING US
MARCH OF EQUALITY

MARCH OF EQUALITY
EQUAL RIGHT NOW!
VOTE x LA POLITICA
THAT IS IMPORTANT, AS THAT'S THE FOUNDATION OF OUR PLATFORM.
THE PEOPLE MUST HEAR WHY THEY SHOULDN'T VOTE FOR THE OPPOSITION, AN IMMORAL PERSON.
20
DAYS LEFT

THE FAKE LUCHADOR.
WHO?
ILLENA CHAVEZ-ESTEVEZ.
ALSO KNOWN AS **ICE**.
DONA ACEVEDO FOR MAYOR
COME ON, I'LL BRING YOU UP TO SPEED AND TELL YOU ALL ABOUT ICE.

THEY SAY SHE SEES YOUR WEAKNESS, THEN PREYS UPON IT.

THEN SHE HAS YOU IN HER GRIP AND MOLDS YOU TO HER WAY OF THINKING. AND THAT'S WHY THERE ARE SO MANY LUCHAS. SHE IS CREATING A RACE WAR.
WITH HER DEMONIC POWERS?

EXPLAIN HOW YOU KNOW THAT.

WELL... SOMETIMES I HAVE THESE DREAMS, THEN IT HAPPENS IN THE FUTURE. WE ALREADY HAD THIS CONVER-SATION. I WAS JUST SPEEDING IT UP.

SANTA...
WHEN YOU HAVE THESE PREMONITIONS, YOU TELL ME, OK?
OK
WHAT IF WE FIGHT HER?
LA POLITICA'S PLATFORM IS FOR THE PEOPLE, FOR US... THAT'S HOW WE'LL BEAT ICE. FOR NOW, LET ME TEACH YOU THE BASICS.
READY!
SIGN IN
VOTE
SIGN UP
Review Script
Handouts
votelapolitica.org
GREAT, LET'S START.
KNOCK KNOCK
DING DONG
SLAM!
WHEN AM I GOING TO LEARN HOW TO FIGHT?

WHEN YOU LEARN YOUR GENERAL ORDERS.
WHAT ARE THOSE?
A SET OF RULES YOU FOLLOW IN THE LINE OF DUTY. THE HONOR YOU LIVE BY.
ALIGN YOUR GENERAL ORDERS WITH YOUR MORALS.
GOT IT.
WHAT'S GENERAL ORDER NUMBER ONE?
WHAT?
PUSH-UPS. NOW.
THIS *ISN'T* FIGHTING.
I KNOW YOU WANT TO LEARN
COMBATIVES. WHAT'S GENERAL ORDER NUMBER THREE?
I DON'T KNOW.
ONE HUNDRED PUSH-UPS.
BLINDFOLDED.
I WANT TO LEARN TO FIGHT.
WHY?
TO PROTECT PEOPLE, LIKE MY MOM DID.
WHAT'S GENERAL ORDER NUMBER FIVE?
ONE... TWO... FIFTY-ONE...

VOTE X
La Politica

COMADRE! I'M DONE. TEACH ME TO FIGHT!
GOOD. COMMIT THEM TO MEMORY.
THIS ISN'T FIGHTING.
IF YOU CAN'T OPERATE YOUR WEAPON, THE WEAPON IS USELESS. NOW TAKE IT APART.

BUT, I DON'T KNOW HOW...

IT WASN'T A QUESTION...
YOU HAVE ONE HOUR.

WHY WOULD THAT VAN BE PARKED OUTSIDE?

HOSPITAL CLOSED
ENTER

DO YOU UNDERSTAND THE PROCEDURE?
THAT'S RIGHT, IT IS IMPORTANT TO SPEAK *WEXAN!*
THE REMOVAL OF GENETIC DEFECTS, LIKE YOURSELF...
¡NO! ¡NO QUIERO ESO!
HOLD HER.
SOME PEOPLE ARE NOTHING BUT BURDENS TO EVERYONE ELSE.
BRING IN THE REST.
THE NEXT DAY
avocado
AND I DON'T KNOW WHERE THEY TOOK HER! IT HAS TO BE RELATED TO THE PINK VAN I SAW.
I'LL TAKE CARE OF IT.
*HOW?!*
I KNOW THEY DID SOMETHING TO HER!
I JUST...
I JUST GET SO... *UGH!*

BAM!
DO THAT AGAIN.
HUH?
ONE, TWO, GO!
PLOP!

TAP!
TAP!
A LA BRAVA, SANTA!

I'M NOT MAD RIGHT NOW...
THAT'S HOW IT WORKS?
I GUESS.
SANTA...
THEY GAVE THE LADY A SHOT TO MAKE HER INFERTILE. IT'S CALLED EUGENICS. THEY STERILIZED HER AND THEN TOOK HER BACK TO THE CAMP WHERE THEY COULD HAVE THEIR WAY WITH HER.

POW!
BAM!
ARGGGH!
WE'LL FIND HER! STOP!

WE'LL MAKE THINGS RIGHT.

OK! WHO'S NEXT ON OUR CAMPAIGN TRAIL?

Chapter 3

AND AS YOUR MAYOR, I WILL CREATE AN ECONOMY THAT WORKS FOR ALL OF US, NOT JUST THE LUCHAS.
EQUAL TREATMENT OF THE POOR...
...OF THE MIDDLE CLASS...

EQUAL TREATMENT AT THE DETENTION CENTER!

HAHA!
HAHA!
HAAA!

WHAT?

HI THERE!
ARE YOU REGISTERED TO VOTE?

OK, I NEED FIFTY SIGNATURES AND I GOT...

VOTE!
1.
2.
3.
4.
5.

BUT HOW'D YOU DO IT, THOUGH?
I TOLD YOU, IT'S MAGIC. I'LL SHOW YOU ANOTHER ONE, READY?
MOM!
PICK A CARD, ANY CARD.
REMEMBER YOUR CARD.

GOT IT.

PUT YOUR CARD FACE DOWN HERE.

NOW, AS WITCHES...
YEAH?

YOU LEARN TO USE THE STARS AS YOUR GUIDE.

THOSE STARS?

YES, AND THEY'LL ALWAYS LEAD YOU HOME. NOW...

THINK OF YOUR CARD.
OK.

NOW, SAY IT THREE TIMES. THAT'S THE RULE.
QUEEN OF HEARTS, QUEEN OF HEARTS, QUEEN OF HEARTS.

MOM, MOM, MOM.
I'M SORRY, MOM. I'LL DO BETTER TOMORROW.

POP!!
GRK!
CRUCK!
KNOK KNOK KLUB
WHAT?! NO!! I'M DRIVING!

I DIDN'T KNOW WE HAD A COMEDY CLUB.
KNOK KNOK KLUB

WE STAND FOR FREE SPEECH!

100% LUCHA CITIZENSHIP!
WHOOOO!
THAT'S RIGHT!

IT'S MY HONOR TO PRESENT OUR NEXT MAYOR, MISS ICE!
LUCHAS, WE HAVE TO FIGHT.
OUR ANCESTORS DIDN'T DIE FIGHTING TO CONQUER THIS NATION—*OUR NATION*—ONLY FOR IT TO BE LOST NOW. WE *MUST* PRESERVE OUR HERITAGE!
GRR!
GRR!
WHOOOO!
GRRRR!
SAY IT WITH ME!
WEXO FOR LUCHAS!
WHAT? NO!
THAT'S RIGHT! WE'RE CAGING THE OUTSIDERS AND *BURNING* THEM TO THE GROUND!

NOOOOO!
NO, THAT'S WRONG!
BURN THEM!
BURN THEM!
STOP!

ARE YOU A MONGREL? WHO DO YOU THINK YOU ARE?
NO, I'M... I'M A XICA, LIKE YOU.
YOUR TYPE, ALWAYS TRYING TO BRING US DOWN TO YOUR LEVEL.
WE CANNOT AND WILL NOT HAVE MONGRELS TAKE OUR JOBS FROM LUCHAS.
GRAB HER.

WHAT? I'M WEXAN! I WAS BORN HERE!

NOTHING CAN SAVE YOU, OR YOUR FAMILY, FOR THAT MATTER, FROM WHERE YOU'RE GOING.
NOOOOO!

BAMMM!
THUD
HMM, I'M SURE YOUR MOTHER WOULD HATE TO SEE YOU LIKE THIS.
WHAT?
PERHAPS SHE DIED ON PURPOSE SO SHE WOULDN'T HAVE TO BE AROUND YOU.
TAKE CARE OF HER.
CLICK
WHAM!
SLAP!
POW!
THUD
BAM!
HOLD ON!!

VROOM!
I FIGURE THIS IS THE SAFEST PLACE, IN CASE THEY COME LOOKING FOR ME.
RUCA, CAN YOU WATCH OUT FOR MY FAMILY?
YOU DON'T LIVE HERE?
UH-UH.
THEN WHO LIVES H—
I GOTTA GO. STAY OUT OF TROUBLE, CHICA.
THANKS FOR YOUR HELP TONIGHT.
...THEN RUCA SAVED ME.
YOU'RE AN UNUSUAL FIGHTER, SANTA.
YOU HAVE LA MANO DE CIELO.
I THINK IT'S THE ONLY REASON YOU'VE STAYED ALIVE THIS LONG.
WHAT?!

IT MEANS SOMEONE IS LOOKING OUT FOR YOU UP THERE.
YOUR GENERAL ORDERS WILL HELP TAME YOUR...BRAWLING MENTALITY. ¿COMPRENDES?
YEAH
TAKE IT APART.
BUT NANA...
NANA TOLD ME MY MOM DIED FR-FROM A GUN BULLET.
YOUR MOM WAS A HERO, SANTA. SHE LOVED YOU A WHOLE LOT, OK?
THERE IS NOTHING TO FEAR IF YOU UNDERSTAND IT.
OKAY...
I'LL TEACH YOU EVERYTHING YOU NEED TO KNOW.
ASÍ.
A WEAPON SHOULD ONLY BE IN THE HANDS OF SOMEONE WHO UNDERSTANDS THE GRAVITY OF WHAT IT CAN DO.

Chapter 4
Ice Cream

HEY!
YOU'RE SANTA, RIGHT?
YEAH.

THANKS FOR SIGNING UP!

ALL COOL LAST NIGHT?
YEAH. COMADRE WAS TEACHING ME DEFENSE.

SHE TEACH YOU ABOUT BLADES?

YOU DIDN'T GIVE ME A CHANCE!

AHH!

YOU SHOULD LEARN TO RUN.
HAVE HER TEACH YOU THAT.

THAT'S NOT FAIR. I WASN'T READY!

CHICA, ANYTHING CAN HAPPEN. YOU HAVE TO GO MEXICAN STYLE. *A LA BRAVA!*

LATER THAT NIGHT
VOTE X La Politica

THANKS FOR YOUR SUPPORT!

WHAT ARE YOU WATCHING?

NEWS REPORT

THE LUCHA CANDIDATE, ICE...
NEWS

...HAS ASKED THE GOOD PEOPLE TO BOYCOTT NON-LUCHA-RUN BUSINESSES.
SHE SAID, ABOUT THE RECENT BOYCOTT, "LUCHA LIVES MATTER."

IT'S GETTING WORSE. WE HAVE TO MAKE SURE PEOPLE VOTE.

KNOCK!
KNOCK!
I'LL JUST LEAVE SOME INFO FOR YOU.

SPLAT!
AY!

GET OUT OF HERE, MONGREL!
WEXO FOR LUCHAS!

NANA!

THEY DON'T LIKE ME.

YOU KNOW WHAT YOU NEED?
MY MOM?

SHE'S ALREADY WITH YOU.

WHAT YOU NEED IS FIDEO Y PAN DULCE. I'M GOING TO THE MARKET.

Z Z Z
HURRY!
CLANK
SPLASH!
WHOOOSSHHH
NANA!
NANA?
MIJA, THERE'S A LOT OF SMOKE OUTSIDE. WHERE'S NANA?
SHE WENT TO THE MARKET!

PLEASE HELP MY GRANDMA! SHE'S INSIDE!
I'M SORRY.
THEY LOCKED THE DOORS. NO ONE GOT OUT IN TIME.
SIR!
NEWS TV
A WEEK HAS NOW PASSED WITH NO LEADS OR ARRESTS OF THE AROCHO MERCADO FIRE.
CLICK!
KNOCK KNOCK
YOU CAN'T SLEEP ALL DAY AND ALL NIGHT ANYMORE.
WHY NOT?
REMEMBER WHEN YOU WERE SICK AND THE DOCTORS DIDN'T KNOW WHY?
YEAH. I WAS IN BED WITH A FEVER AND I COULDN'T MOVE.
WHAT MADE YOU BETTER WAS THE LOVE THAT SURROUNDED YOU.
IT WAS YOUR MOM WHO CURED YOU.

TELL ME THE TRUTH. TELL ME THE TRUTH. TELL ME THE TRUTH.
I'M SORRY. THERE IS NOTHING MORE I CAN DO.
SHE'S TOO FAR GONE.
I'LL SEE MYSELF OUT.
I NEED TO SPEAK TO GENERAL ROSARIO MEJIA.
IT'S AN EMERGENCY.
LET ME.
I'LL TAKE CARE OF THE REST.
MY LITTLE GIRL.
GIVE HER THE STRENGTH TO SURVIVE. GIVE HER THE STRENGTH TO SURVIVE. GIVE HER THE STRENGTH TO SURVIVE.
I'M ALWAYS WITH YOU, SANTA.

THEY'RE HERE.
TELL THEM TO HURRY. SHE'LL WAKE SOON.
BOOP
BOOP
BOOOO
ROSARIO MEJIA
GLORIA MEJIA, AFFECTIONATELY KNOWN AS NANA, WILL FOREVER BE IN OUR HEARTS AND MEMORIES. SHE IS SURVIVED BY–
GET OUT OF HERE!
SPLAT!
GASP!
GASP!
GRRR

GO BACK TO YOUR HUTS, MONGRELS!
SANTA!!
GRRRRRRRA!!!!
STUPID, FILTHY...
MONGRRRRELLLLLL
BAM!
ARRGGHHH!
POW!!
AY!
STOP! STOP! MERCY!
THAT'S ENOUGH, SANTA!
LET'S GO BACK TO NANA, ¿SÍ?

Chapter 5

BACK OF THE BUS FOR YOU.

SEAT'S TAKEN.

READY TO VOTE TOMORROW?

1
DAY LEFT

THIS PLACE HAS THE BEST TRES LECHES.

HI, CAN WE HAVE SOME SERVICE?

WHAT'S YOUR FIFTH GENERAL ORDER?
UPHOLD THE BILL OF RIGHTS AT ALL COSTS. WHY?
DO YOU KNOW THEM?
GET OUT! WE DON'T SERVE YOU PEOPLE!
FREEDOM OF SPEECH.
ARE YOU LISTENING? OR IS YOUR BRAIN TOO SMALL TO UNDERSTAND LUCHA TALK?
PROTECTION OF LIFE, LIBERTY, AND PROSPERITY. THE RIGHT TO REMAIN SILENT.
YOU THINK THIS IS FUNNY, HUH?
HEY!
SANTA?
THE RIGHT TO BEAR ARMS.
YOU THINK THAT UP THERE...
LA POLITICA 51%
ICE 49%
WE WON? WE WON!!
MEANS NOTHIN'! ICE SAID ALL MONGRELS GONNA BE TAKEN IN.
AMENDMENT NINE: ALL RIGHTS UNWRITTEN ARE STILL THE PEOPLE'S RIGHTS.
NOT THE GOVERNMENT'S.
VERY NICE, SANTA.

HOW'S THAT FOR A RULE?

POW!

YOU'RE UNDER ARREST!
FOR WHAT?

DISTURBING THE PEACE.

WE HAVE TO FIND OUT WHERE THEY'RE TAKING HER.

ACROSS TOWN
RESTRICTED
KEEP OUT

VOTE × La Politica
WHAT DO YOU MEAN YOU LOST THEM?
I-I WAS WITH THEM AND THEY TOLD ME TO GO HOME.
SO YOU DID? YOU COULDA CALLED ME.

DONA ACEVEDO
THANKS FOR YOUR TIME HERE. I WISH YOU WELL.
THANK YOU, EVERYONE, FOR COMING! I'M THE MAYOR OF WEXO BECAUSE OF YOUR VOTES...

IT'S JUST THAT THEY WERE FIGHTING US...
...AND WE HAVE TO PROTECT THE SWEET.
THAT'S RIGHT. WE NEED TO FIND OUT THE LOCATION OF THE DETENTION CENTER...
AND WHAT, BREAK IN? I CAN'T. I'M THE MAYOR AND I HAVE TO PROVE I'M THEIR VOICE, NOT JUST BRAWN.
CRASH!
THE REASON PEOPLE AREN'T BEHIND YOU IS BECAUSE YOU'RE NOT BEHIND THEM.
COME ON. YOU BOTH CAN STAY AT MY PLACE.
FLASH
SORRY, IT'S FOR A PROJECT.
WHAT PROJECT?
THE TRUE HISTORY OF WEXO.
IF WE DON'T CHANGE THE NARRATIVE, WHO WILL, YOU KNOW?
CONGRATS ON YOUR WIN, MAYOR.
I HOPE YOU—AND NOT JUST THE LUCHAS—WRITE THE HISTORY BOOKS.

YOU CAN'T HIDE FOREVER, MONGREL.
TSSSSSSSS!
POW!
*GASP!*
YOU'RE MINE!
AHHH!
ARE YOU ALL RIGHT?
IT WAS ANOTHER ONE OF MY DREAMS.
WHAT DO YOU MEAN?
LIKE THE PREMONITIONS YOU SAID I HAD.
WE WERE FIGHTING THE LUCHAS. WHEREVER WE WERE, THE CEILING WAS REALLY HIGH.
LIKE, YOU CAN FIT AN AIRPLANE HIGH?
YEAH. AND RUCA WAS THERE.
RUCA?

OK, ACCORDING TO YOUR DESCRIPTION, THE DETENTION CAMP IS AT A HANGAR, AND THE ONLY HANGAR IN TOWN IS THE OLD MILITARY ONE.

THERE ARE ENTRANCES HERE AND HERE. THERE'S A GUARD AT THE VEHICLE ENTRANCE. REMEMBER THE RULES OF ENGAGEMENT?

DON'T ENGAGE UNLESS ENGAGED. GET IN, GET OUT. IF YOU HAVE TO FIRE, SELF-DEFENSE ONLY.

ELIMINATE TARGETS. PRESERVE CIVILIANS. CHECK.

IF WE DIVIDE AND CONQUER...

ANYONE WANT A CAFECITO?

DIVIDE AND CONQUER, HUH?

YOU'RE GONNA NEED PEOPLE.

I CAN HELP!

LEAVE IT TO ME.

WE'LL NEED PEOPLE ON THE FRONT LINES.

MOVE IT, MONGREL!
MOVE!

SECURED PERSONNEL ONLY. TURN AROUND.
I'M COMADRE DE LEON, FIRST SERGEANT OF THE UNITED STATES ARMY.

WE'D LIKE TO SPEAK TO WHO'S IN CHARGE.

# Chapter 6

YOU DON'T HAVE ACCESS TO THIS BASE, MA'AM!
WE'RE NOT ASKING FOR ACCESS. I'D LIKE TO SPEAK TO WHO'S IN CH—
SLAM!
WE HAVE A SITUATION HERE.
ARGGHHH
VIVA LA RAZA!
GRRRRR
BAM!
VIVA LA RAZA!

MY FRIEND IS IN THERE AND SHE'S GONNA DIE IF I DON'T SAVE HER.
WHAT?
RUCA. IN THE DREAM. I DIDN'T TELL YOU?
WHAT'S THIS NONSENSE HERE?
UMM, WE'RE TAKING YOU DOWN.
RIGHT. YOU AND WHAT ARMY?
VIVA LA-
SETTLE DOWN, MONGRELS!
VIVA LA RAZA!
VIVA LA RAZA!
STOP THAT RIGHT NOW!
RAZA!

***GREAT!*** THERE'S ROOM FOR ALL OF YOU IN HERE. YOU'LL DISAPPEAR.

THAT'S THE ***WEXAN*** WAY!

***NO!*** IT'S NOT THE WEXAN—

LET'S START WITH YOU...

VIVA LA RAZA!

HOW ARE YOU GONNA FIGHT?!
THE WAY WE ALWAYS DO.
VIVA!
VIVA
LA...
LA...
TST
TST
MEXICAN
STYLE!
RAZA!
BAM!
GRRR!
CRASH

CRASH
I BROUGHT SOME SUPPORTERS!
HA! HA! HA!
WHAT ARE THEY GONNA DO? DIE?
FIND OUT, WASI'CHU.
BAM!
ARGHHH!
POW!
BAM!
GUARDS!

I GOT THIS! GO, SAVE THE PEOPLE INSIDE!
SLAM!

TSSSSSS!
AHHH!! I CAN'T SEE!

EEEEEEEE!

I DON'T HAVE TIME FOR THIS. GET HER!
POW!
AHHHH!
I TRIED.

WHACK!
¡VÁMONOS!

WE NEED TO BE OUT THERE FIGHTING!
RUCA! THERE YOU ARE!

RUCA, WAIT.

REMEMBER WHEN YOU WERE LEARNING SPANISH AND YOU THOUGHT *RUCA* MEANT ROCK?
AND NOT ONE OF YOU TOLD ME FOR YEARS. THAT WAS MESSED UP.

I WASN'T THE BEST TO YOU. I KNOW THAT. BUT YOU'RE STRONG.

NEVER STOP FIGHTING FOR WHAT'S RIGHT.

EVERYONE LOOKS UP TO YOU. YOU'RE OUR RUCA.

I WILL ALWAYS LOVE YOU.
GIVE HER HER JUSTICE. GIVE HER HER JUSTICE. GIVE HER HER JUSTICE.
*GASP*
NO, DON'T!
MOM, PLEASE DON'T LEAVE ME!

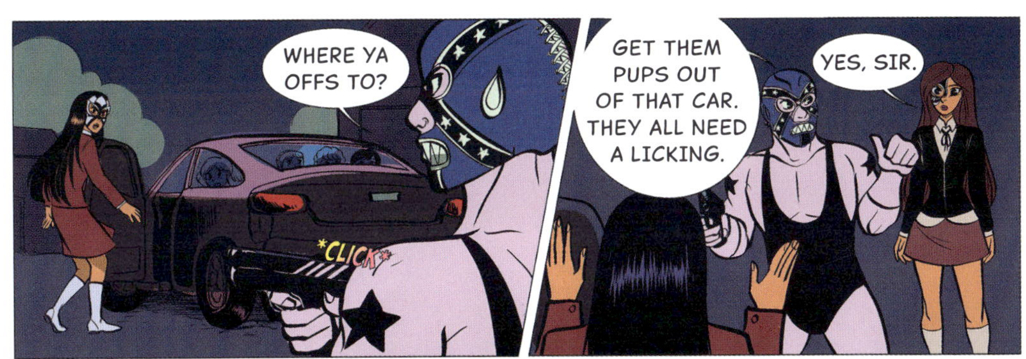

YOU HAD TO START A RUCKUS.

YOU HAD TO IMPRISON US WITHOUT CAUSE!

YOU KILLED YOUR MOM.
NO!
THEN WHY ARE YOU ALIVE AND SHE'S DEAD?
HIT ME!
NO!
BAM!
I CAN'T HIT YOU.
BAHAHA! STUPID GIRL.
POW!
OOMPH
RAHHH!
YOU DESERVE A SLOW AND PAINFUL DEATH.

EITHER WAY, I WIN. YOU BECOME HATE, I BECOME A PART OF YOU.
YOU DIE, EVEN BETTER.

SANTA!
MOM, YOU'RE BACK!

OF COURSE I AM. I'D NEVER LEAVE YOU.

LOOK, MOM, I STILL HAVE YOUR NECKLACE!
AND IT WORKED!
GREAT.

BUT I NEED TO LEARN MY POWERS NOW.

THERE'S THIS BULLY WHO KEEPS TAKING THIS GIRL'S FOOD. I NEED TO PROTECT HER.
YES, YOU DO.

YOU LOOK THE BULLY IN THE EYES.
I CAN DO THAT.
THEN YOU LOOK INSIDE HER AND TALK IN LANGUAGE SHE UNDERSTANDS.

IF YOU NEED MY HELP, YOU CAN ALWAYS TAP INTO ME HERE.

THAT'S NOT A POWER, MOM.
IT IS. YOU JUST HAVE TO KNOW HOW TO USE IT.

I'M ALWAYS WITH YOU, SANTA

YOU MONGRELS DON'T HAVE THE CAPACITY TO LEARN.
WE, WEXANS, ARE THE FUTURE!
*PUNCH ME, MIJA!*
RAAAHHH!
ZSHHH

DRIP
DRIP
THANK YOU SO MUCH FOR COMING OUT. I AM PROUD TO SAY THAT WEXO IS A LAND OF IMMIGRANTS.
THEIR STORY, MY STORY, OUR STORY, IS ROOTED IN FAMILY AND FUELED BY HOPE.
OUR STORIES CONTINUE TODAY— ALL ACROSS WEXO.
DONA ACEVEDO
CONGRATULATIONS
MAYOR
La Politica

THE COURT RULES IN FAVOR OF THE PLAINTIFF. REPARATIONS OF THE FORCED STERILIZATION...

I SHOULD GET GOING.
WHERE?
HOME. GOT A FEW THINGS TO TAKE CARE OF.

TAKE CARE OF THIS FOR ME.

YUP. THINGS ARE LOOKING UP.

PURRRRRRRRRR
THE END

# About the Author

**KAYDEN PHOENIX** IS A WRITER FROM LOS ANGELES, CALIFORNIA. SHE CREATED THE FIRST LATINA SUPERHERO TEAM IN COMIC BOOK HISTORY: A LA BRAVA. "A BIG PART OF MY LIFE'S PURPOSE IS TO GIVE VOICE TO STORIES AS MULTIFACETED, ATYPICAL, AND DIVERSE AS THE PEOPLE WE FIND IN THE REAL WORLD."